# WAYNETTA AND THE CORNSTALK

## A Texas Fairy Tale

Helen Ketteman

Illustrated by **Diane Greenseid**

Albert Whitman & Company, Chicago, Illinois

For Baby Amitsis; Lucy Bashforth; Shannon and Baby Freeman;
Ally and Ben Fuhs; Huck, Tyrone, and Ella Green; Mia and Elle Green;
Adam Reardon; Nathalie and Maialen Soltvedt; Jack Westdijk,
and Corinna Won. —H.K.

For my gigantically wonderful nieces and nephews, with love. —D.G.

**Also by Helen Ketteman**
*Armadilly Chili*
*Not Yet, Yvette*
*Señorita Gordita*
*The Three Little Gators*

Library of Congress Cataloging-in-Publication Data
Ketteman, Helen.
Waynetta and the cornstalk : a Texas fairy tale / by Helen Ketteman ; illustrated by Diane Greenseid.
p. cm.
Summary: A retelling of "Jack and the Beanstalk" which features a Texas cowgirl, a magic cornstalk, and a giant cowboy in the clouds.
ISBN 13: 978-0-8075-8687-7 (hardcover)
ISBN 13: 978-0-8075-8688-4 (paperback)
[1. Fairy tales. 2. Giants—Folklore. 3. Cowboys—Folklore. 4. Folklore—England.] I. Greenseid, Diane, ill. II. Jack and the beanstalk. English. III. Title.
PZ8.K474Way 2007 398.2—dc22[E] 2006023397

The design is by Carol Gildar.

For information about Albert Whitman & Company, please visit our web site at www.albertwhitman.com.

**nce,** a whip of a girl named Waynetta lived with her ma on a ranch in the poorest, scrubbiest part of Texas. They worked hard as eight-legged mules, but barely scraped by.

One long dry summer, the well bottomed out, the pastures dried up, and the longhorn cattle got so thin it took three of them standing together to cast a shadow. Waynetta and her ma had to sell off the longhorns until only one was left.

Finally, Ma gave up altogether. "We've run out of money to buy feed, Waynetta. You'd best sell that last critter 'fore it starves." Waynetta headed out with the longhorn.

After a while, she met a stranger.

"Howdy, Missy!" he said. "Where're you taking that sorry-looking critter?"

"I aim to sell him," Waynetta answered.

"Hows about tradin' him for a handful of magic corn?" asked the stranger.

"Magic corn?" asked Waynetta. "What does it do?"

"These corn kernels will bring you good luck, little lady."

"We sure could use some luck," Waynetta said. "It's a deal!"

When she got home, Waynetta dropped the kernels in Ma's hands. "Look!" she said with a grin. "Magic corn!"

Ma frowned. "You must be chuckle-headed, girl. The only magic this corn's got is the disappearin' kind." She tossed them out the window.

Waynetta felt lower than a coyote in a canyon. How could she make it up to Ma?

The next morning, Waynetta looked out the window. A giant cornstalk blocked the sun! She hurried outside.

"That looks like magic to me," she said, "and I aim to find some luck." She started climbing.

When she broke through the clouds, Waynetta could hardly believe her eyes! There was the biggest ranch she'd ever seen. She walked to the front door. It was so huge, she could barely reach over the doorstep. She gathered her courage and knocked.

A giant woman opened the door.

"Why, you're purty as a bluebonnet! Where'd you come from?"

"I climbed a giant cornstalk, Ma'am," answered Waynetta.

The giant woman picked up Waynetta. "I reckon you've come to take back the things my husband stole from your ma years ago."

She set Waynetta on a giant-sized table. "You'd best have a bite to eat. And be careful, darlin'. My husband's a mean one."

Waynetta was chowing down on a great big chicken-fried steak when a loud, angry voice called:

"Fee, fie, foe, fat,
I think I smell a cowgirl brat!
Fee, fie, foe, feet,
chicken-fried cowgirl is what
I'll eat!"

"Hide!" the giant woman whispered.

Waynetta hid behind a bowl of beans just as the giant stomped into the room.

The giant yanked open a pantry door. Out strolled a long-horn no bigger than a barn cat. He stroked its ear, and a golden cowpat fell to the floor. "I love gold!" the giant shouted.

Next he took out a teeny lariat and whirled it backwards over his head. He looped it around a thimble-sized bucket. "I love this rope! It never misses!"

Finally he tilted the tiny bucket over a huge tub. Water poured into the tub, filling it. "I love that bucket! It never runs out of water!"

He dropped the rope on the floor, looped the bucket around his pinkie, and climbed in the tub to soak. Soon, he fell asleep.

Waynetta took a deep breath. "With those things and some hard work, Ma and I can make our own luck!"

Waynetta climbed off the table and tiptoed to the tub. She picked up the lariat and lassoed the longhorn. But when she tried to slip the bucket off the giant's pinkie, he woke up.

Waynetta hightailed it to the cornstalk and scrambled to the ground where Ma was waiting.

Ma gasped. "Why, that looks like my little longhorn missing all these years!" She rubbed its ear and sure enough, a golden cowpat fell to the ground.

"It's him, Ma," said Waynetta. "Now we can buy a new herd of cattle."

"Waynetta, darlin'," said Ma. "Sometimes I wonder if that taco brain of yours is a bit short of fillin'. Gold or no gold, we can't raise cattle without water."

"That's why I'm going back up, Ma—to get the magic bucket!"

Waynetta hid the lariat under her hat and climbed the cornstalk again. The giant's wife let her in. "I need that bucket, Ma'am," said Waynetta.

The giant woman nodded. "Be extra careful. My husband's mad as a fire ant!"

From the hallway, the giant's voice thundered:

"Fee, fie, foe, fin,
I smell that cowgirl brat agin!
Fee, fie, foe, fits,
I'll cook myself some cowgirl grits!"

As the giant stormed into the kitchen, Waynetta ran right between his boots and grabbed the bucket.

"Well, if it ain't the seasoning for my grits!" the giant shouted. He stomped after her.

Waynetta raced to the cornstalk. She was almost there when the giant grabbed her. "I feel hungry and you look tasty!" he roared.

Waynetta whirled the lariat. "Do your stuff, rope!" She lassoed the giant's nose and tugged hard.

**"Arrrgggghhh!"** yelled the giant, dropping Waynetta.

Waynetta leapt on the cornstalk. The giant climbed after her!

"Fee, fie, foe, fow,
    that cowgirl brat has had it now!
Fee, fie, foe, few,
    that cowgirl's gon' be barbecue!"

Ma was waiting on the ground with the ax. "Bridle your jaw, Mister!" she shouted. "That cowgirl's my daughter!" The instant Waynetta leapt off the cornstalk, Ma swung the ax, and in three strong blows, chopped the cornstalk down.

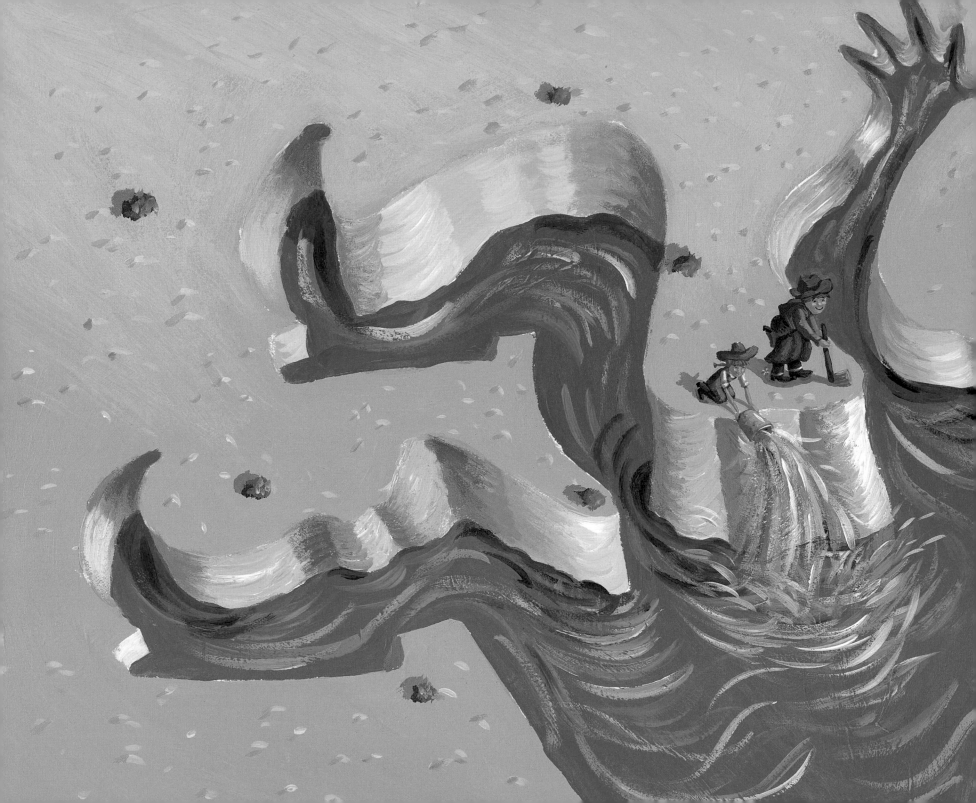

THWUNK! The giant crashed to the ground, making a deep giant-shaped hole.

Waynetta tipped the bucket over the hole. "I hope that giant can swim," she said. In no time, the hole became a fine lake.

With plenty of water, grass grew
on the ranch once again. With the golden
cow patties, Waynetta and her ma bought a
new herd of longhorns.

   As for the giant, he bonked his head so hard
in the fall, it knocked the mean right out of him.
He and his wife stayed on the ranch and worked
alongside Waynetta and her ma . . .

and they all lived happy as junebugs ever after.